BELINDA IN THE POOL

A SHORT STORY OF FAMILY DISTURBANCE

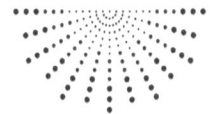

DOUGLAS CLEGG

ALKEMARA
PRESS

Disclaimer:

Belinda in the Pool is a work of fiction. Names, places, characters
and incidents are a product of the author's imagination. Any
resemblance to actual locales, events, or persons, living or dead, is
entirely coincidental.

PRAISE FOR DOUGLAS CLEGG'S FICTION

"Clegg's stories can chill the spine so effectively that the reader should keep paramedics on standby."
—Dean Koontz, *New York Times* bestselling author.

"Douglas Clegg has become the new star in horror fiction."
—Peter Straub, *New York Times* bestselling author of *Ghost Story* and, with Stephen King, *The Talisman*

"Douglas Clegg is the best horror novelist of the post-Stephen King generation."
— Bentley Little, *USA Today* bestselling author of *The Haunted*.

"Clegg gets high marks on the terror scale…"
—*The Daily News (New York)*

ALSO BY DOUGLAS CLEGG

STAND-ALONE NOVELS

Afterlife

Breeder

The Children's Hour

Dark of the Eye

Goat Dance

The Halloween Man

The Hour Before Dark

Mr. Darkness

Naomi

Neverland

You Come When I Call You

NOVELLAS & SHORT NOVELS

The Attraction

The Dark Game (Two Novelettes)

Dinner with the Cannibal Sisters

Isis

The Necromancer

Purity

The Words

SERIES

THE HARROW SERIES

Nightmare House, Book 1

Mischief, Book 2

The Infinite, Book 3

The Abandoned, Book 4

The Necromancer (Prequel Novella)

Isis (Prequel Novella)

THE CRIMINALLY INSANE SERIES

Bad Karma, Book 1

Red Angel, Book 2

Night Cage, Book 3

THE VAMPYRICON TRILOGY

The Priest of Blood, Book 1

The Lady of Serpents, Book 2

The Queen of Wolves, Book 3

THE CHRONICLES OF MORDRED

Mordred, Bastard Son (Book 1)

COLLECTIONS

Lights Out: Collected Stories

Night Asylum

The Nightmare Chronicles

Wild Things

BOX SET BUNDLES

Bad Places (3 Novels)

Coming of Age (3 Dark Novellas)

Dark Rooms (3 Novels)

Criminally Insane: The Series (3 Novels)

Halloween Chillers

Harrow: Three Novels (Books 1-3)

Harrow: Four Novels (Books 1-4)

Haunts (8 Novel Box Set)

Lights Out (3 Collection Box Set)

Night Towns (3 Novels)

The Vampyricon Trilogy (3 Novels)

With more new novels, novellas and stories to come.

GET THE NEWSLETTER

Get book updates, exclusive offers, news of contests & special treats for readers—become a V.I.P. member of Douglas Clegg's long-running free newsletter.

Subscribe at DouglasClegg.com/newsletter

BELINDA IN THE POOL

S itting just in front of Michael and his daughter, the woman — white of hair and coat — lifted her card.

"Three hundred!" the auctioneer said. "Number 17!"

"If she'd just quit bidding," Belinda said, under her breath.

Michael — *Number 5* — glared at the back of the annoying whiteness of Number 17. Belinda gave him a nudge. He held up his card.

Twenty people in sweaters and coats sat on hard plastic chairs crammed into the cold, dusty little shop.

Belinda squeezed his arm. "You can get it, Dad."

Nobody's going much over 500 dollars for this, Michael thought. It wasn't even worth three hundred to anyone in the market for antique watches with silver bands.

In that second between his most recent bid and the auctioneer's next mouthing, Michael tasted something bitter at the back of his throat.

After years of searching, here we are, he thought.

In a junk shop with Belinda, a twenty-minute drive door-to-door, the watch right there in front of them

"Your mother's not going to be happy," he said. "I wasn't even supposed to go over two-fifty. Holy cow."

"But we're almost there," Belinda said. "And it's just money. You'll make more. You always say that."

His daughter — verbally expressive beyond her fourteen years, curious, inquisitive, advanced in her thinking — constantly surprised him. Belinda of the dark hair, slightly bowed shoulders, fresh-faced, the last of summer's freckles still faint on her cheek, green pond-water eyes, unremarkable nose, barest hint of mascara, vanishing dimple at her chin, most of the baby fat gone now, at the beginning of her swan years, a little silver crescent moon on a slim chain around her neck, fog-gray wool sweater pulled over orange T-shirt above blue jeans, fake tattoo — *the Eye of Horus* — at the back of her hand; she of the swim team, of the annual Charlotte Russe made with the flourish of a great chef abandoning messy pans and spattered bowls in her wake, of sweet crushes on pretty male pop idols with wavy hair who posed in posters tacked up around her bedroom, of the little squeal of delight in sampling gelato at a shop on the *Via di San Simone*, of the amusement park obsession, of the junior debate team, of the long chess games with her old man where they talked endlessly of the world and school and how things used to be and how they were now, of the trips to Spain and England and Italy, of the bruised knees made better by a father's kiss, of the treasure hunts, of the late night movie marathons with stove-hot popcorn dripping in butter and parmesan; so much like her mother and so much unlike her, too.

And Belinda in the pool, Michael thought, suddenly cold.

"Dad, don't let anyone else get it. It's meant for you. I can feel it."

The woman in white raised her arm again, yellow card in hand.

WHEN THE AUCTION WAS OVER, Michael and his daughter remained in their chairs, waiting out rush hour traffic.

Belinda passed him a mint from the small flat tin she kept in her pocket.

"Sorry, Dad."

"Sometimes you win, sometimes you lose," he said.

"That's what losers say."

"Very funny."

He thought he might tell her, right then, about why that watch meant so much.

But why should she be burdened with his reasons? Belinda was still a baby in his eyes, despite her womanly form emerging, *oh god*, he thought, *here come the breasts*, her waistline narrowing as hips curved and legs lengthened; and the way her hair sparkled after she'd brushed it; the strange silences during which he imagined her a captive in some newly minted cell of that hormonal prison called adolescence, unable — suddenly — to talk openly about private feelings.

It came back to him as he sat there, a thud at his heart, the nightmare moment — those dreadful few seconds earlier that week when the reality hit him.

Somehow, it made the search for the watch that much more important.

HE'D DRIVEN over to pick her up at the YMCA. Tired of waiting in the parking lot, Michael went inside and passed through the men's locker room and on through doors into the swimming area.

He stood by folded bleachers, checking the clock on the wall to make sure he wasn't early.

Belinda emerged from restless water and ascended the metal ladder at the edge of the pool. She wore a midnight blue bathing suit, her skin glistening. She'd only just drawn off her bathing cap, unleashing a cascade of thick, shiny hair that curved along her still-tanned shoulders.

At that moment, Michael became aware of the boys.

All those seventeen and eighteen year olds standing by the edge of the pool, towels flung over shoulders, their tell-all *Speedos*, mouths agape, eyes burning with intensity, an electrical, musky charge in the chlorinated air as they watched his daughter in a way that disturbed Michael to no end, bringing a memory of things best forgotten, mistakes made.

Of what it felt like to be them.

Oh god, Belinda. Not yet.

He could feel her slipping from his grasp. She'd be under the waves, carried by dangerous currents to some distant shore he'd never reach. No more gelato with dad, no more squandering of Saturdays in junk shops, no more buttery, cheesy popcorn, no more Michael-Belinda Misadventures.

And something further in that moment at the pool.

Something that came from Belinda herself.

A gleam of triumph.

He tried to push the moment from his mind.

MICHAEL LOOKED down at his yellow card with the number 5 scrawled on it in magic marker. He passed it to her.

"A souvenir."

"Yee-haw." She folded up the card until it fit in the palm of her hand.

"Come on, it's been fun," he said. "Not a bad way to spend an afternoon off."

Belinda slumped further down in her chair. "There's absolutely no other watch you want in the entire world?"

"Sounds silly when you put it like that."

The shopkeeper's son began sweeping the floor around empty chairs. The boy — roughly fifteen, Michael guessed — glanced at Belinda and smiled.

"He's not very smart," Belinda whispered, leaning in close. She smelled of French soap and raspberries. "Look. He's doubling his work. You clear chairs first, then sweep."

"You should tell him."

"Like I care."

Belinda moved her legs to the right to avoid the broom. She didn't look at the boy. She swiveled in her chair. Her knees brushed against her father's. Instinctively, Michael pulled his legs away.

"Makes me angry," she said, after a full minute. "That lady just grabbed what's supposed to be yours."

"I was outbid."

"No, she grabbed it. It can't possibly mean as much to her — not like it does to you. Just look at her."

He turned his attention to the far right, beyond the chairs.

The couple that ran the shop sat on one side of a long narrow table. The lucky bidders took the chair directly across, one at a time, signing checks and paperwork.

Passed across the table: a 19th century painting of an old mill by a stream surrounded by a chipped ornate frame, a little bronze art deco goddess Diana with bow in hand, two giant blue and green glass globes, the small cast-iron table with pink marble top, a doll with its face pushed in and its companion dollhouse without doors, a moth-eaten full-length mink, a small cardboard box filled with what Belinda had called "old lady jewelry," and a few other things that Michael mostly considered crap.

And then, the woman of white, receiving a little square box passed from the owner.

MICHAEL COULDN'T SEE what she did — her back

was toward him — but guessed that she opened the box and drew out the watch.

Belinda arched her back, stretching out. "You could've bid more."

"Your mother would kill me."

"But this is the one time we actually found it," she said.

"It's just a watch. It doesn't really matter."

"If you want it, it matters."

"Sometimes it's good to want something but not get it."

"Yeah, except you never get what you want," she said. "Remember Italy? Your boring old conference was over. You wanted to go to Florence. Mom wanted two more days in Rome. Mom won. We stayed in Rome. And you told me you'd wanted to go to the Uffizi since you were in college."

"Well, we had a good time," Michael said. "And we can always go back."

"But we won't. You only go where work sends you. You never take a vacation just for you. And you won't ever see the Uffizi. Let's just write that little dream off."

"Well, I say we'll go again," he said. "Someday. Florence ain't going anywhere."

"You never know," she said. "A war. A tsunami. A world cataclysm. Things happen. I'm betting a couple thousand years ago somebody put off a summer trip to Pompeii and then — well, the whole Vesuvius thing."

"You're a little too smart for your old man."

"It's just that things only come around once. Sometimes."

"It's just a watch."

"Is it?"

Belinda crossed and uncrossed her legs. She tapped her foot against the empty chair in front, kicking it just enough that the chair moved forward.

"I don't know if I want to live in the same universe where that lady gets the watch and you don't," Belinda whispered as she glanced around. "It's an injustice."

He wasn't sure, but it looked like her eyes shone with tears.

He reached over and hugged her. She pressed her face against his shoulder.

"Aw, come on," he whispered. "Sometimes the hunt's better than the treasure."

Belinda drew back, a glint of tear at her cheek. She wiped it away. The Eye of Horus, now a smudge on the back of her hand.

"I wanted you to get it," she said.

"Me, too."

"It's not fair."

"Life's never fair." He kissed her on the forehead. "And it's not all about me, anyway. But you've got to be the sweetest kid on the planet to stick up for your old man. We'll find that watch someday."

"And someday you'll see the Uffizi Gallery," she said, with a slow drip of cynicism.

The shopkeepers' son began clearing chairs away. Again, the boy glanced over at his daughter.

"See? He's going to have to sweep all over again," Belinda said, momentarily distracted from her mood. "If he'd done it right the first time…"

Michael closed his eyes, not wanting to observe the boy's glance at his daughter, the up and down of his eyes.

DON'T THINK of the pool.

But the blue water bubbled up behind his eyes, the dark of imagination lightened into the gymnasium pool, then an unfamiliar siren rose from its depths while all those innocent and terrible boys groveled in a way that seemed obscene and pure and primal.

Look away.

He glanced at the back of his wrist, then up to the wall where the clock should've been.

In its place, *a giant Eye of Horus stared at him as if in judgment.*

"Dad, Dad — look, quick," Belinda said, as if she were waking him to an emergency.

Michael opened his eyes.

BELINDA TURNED HALFWAY and pointed toward the large window facing the street.

The woman of whiteness stood at the edge of the sidewalk, glancing one way and then the other, waiting for a gap in the heavy traffic.

She stepped off the curb only to be chased back to the sidewalk by a car.

"They need to put more traffic lights downtown," Belinda said. "Big accident last week right out there."

"There was?" Michael said.

"It was on the news. A head-on. *Boom*. Four cars involved. All crushed. Some crazy driver. Probably suicidal."

"Awful."

"Not pretty."

The shop was on a strange corner, jutting out like a peninsula into a choppy sea of streets, heavy traffic bearing down from the interstate less than a mile away.

"She won't get across any time soon," Belinda said. "She should walk down to State Street and then go over at Third or Milton. It's a longer walk but safer. Or wait it out in here until the traffic dies down. Someone should tell her."

Michael watched the back of the woman of white.

"Dad, remember how you're always saying I should take fate in my own hands?"

"Of course. Seize the day."

"You can still get the watch."

"It's too late," he said.

"She's standing right there. She won't be crossing the street anytime soon. There's time. You could offer her fifty bucks more."

Michael stood up to get a better look at the woman on the sidewalk.

Belinda slipped outside and went to stand just behind the woman. She glanced back at her father through the shop window, motioning for him to follow.

"EXCUSE ME," Michael said. "Miss?"

The woman of white didn't look his way at first.

"Hello?" he asked.

She glanced over. Younger than he'd expected, given the white hair.

Belinda stepped up. "My dad just wants to see if he can buy that watch off you."

"I'm sorry," the woman said. "You bid on it, too?"

"We sat right behind you." Belinda brought out

the yellow card from the back pocket of her jeans, unfolding it. "See? Number 5."

The woman looked from Michael's face to his daughter's.

"My daughter, Belinda."

Then, he introduced himself.

The woman of white smiled at Belinda.

"I'm Carolyn. What a beautiful sweater." Then, she looked over at Michael, her smile fading. "I could never give this watch up. You could pull out five thousand dollars cash right now. I wouldn't be able to hand it over. And I'm not rich. I could use five thousand. Couldn't we all."

She raised her wrist to display her win, drawing the coat sleeve back. The silver and turquoise gleamed in the moody slant of November's dimming light.

"It's really a man's watch. Seems old-fashioned to say it. As if watches could be male or female." The woman dragged her sleeve down again. "But I just have to have it. And you must've been my competition."

"My dad's been looking for that exact watch for years," Belinda said.

The woman looked from Belinda to her father. "I'm sorry. Maybe you'll find another one."

Belinda walked behind the woman's back. She mouthed a word that Michael thought might be: "fate," or perhaps, he thought: "hate." Or "wait."

"Sure I can't change your mind?" Michael asked.

The woman held her hand up, a stop sign. "Please leave me alone. I'm sorry you didn't get it, but it's mine. And I don't feel comfortable with you standing right here."

Carolyn turned and looked back toward the shop.

Michael wondered if she might run inside and claim he was harassing her. He had to be sensitive. He took a step back.

"No," he said. "I understand. I'm sorry for bothering you."

Belinda, on the other side of the woman, made a rolling motion with her hands, which Michael interpreted as *keep talking, Dad.*

"Just name a price," he said, worried that the woman might throw out some astronomical figure and then he'd have trouble saving face in front of Belinda.

"Look," the woman said. "Fuck off."

She stepped into the street.

SOMETHING ABOUT BELINDA caught his eye.

His daughter darted to the edge of the curb, a blur of motion reaching for Carolyn's white coat.

In the same second that Belinda did this, a truck

came out of swift traffic, brakes squealing, and slammed into the woman of white at the dead center of her body.

Belinda stepped back to the curb. Instinctively, Michael nearly leapt for his daughter, and they both crumpled down to the sidewalk in each other's arms.

Carolyn flew like a great white bird to the truck's windshield, reaching upward.

The woman of white slid down across the hood and then fell to the street.

MICHAEL RODE WITH THE WOMAN — Carolyn — in the ambulance, after making sure that the police would give Belinda a ride home. He felt responsible. He wondered if he'd scared the woman a little, making her want to get out into the street, away from him, her stalker.

Michael noticed that the sleeves of the woman's coat had torn, but her arms were pristine.

The watch seemed to have survived perfectly well.

AT THE HOSPITAL, Carolyn opened her eyes. He

told her where she was, who he was, and why she couldn't move.

The nurses flitted around the gurney, doctors chattered, someone called for a specialist, someone else called for someone named Bobby, and Michael felt a thud in his chest knowing he had a few seconds before anyone might see.

He thought of Belinda, all those times they'd scoured auctions and shops, looking for a watch he was certain they'd never find.

And then, found.

And lost.

Right here, inches away.

Carolyn's eyes opened, watching him.

He slipped the watch off her wrist and into the pocket of his jacket.

She'll forget this.

After the anesthesia, it'll all be a weird dream to her when she recovers.

LATER, he called his wife and told her what happened — *accident, hospital* — nothing about the watch. She snarled at him for abandoning Belinda to ride with some stranger in an ambulance.

"Who does that?" she kept asking, as if he'd been unfaithful. "And you leave your daughter? After what she just saw? She's only fourteen, Mike."

"What?" he said. "She seemed fine. She said she was fine. She went back to the shop. The police were there. I guess I didn't think clearly. Is something wrong?"

"She's in shock."

"Can I talk to her?"

"I'm not sure she wants to talk to you. I'm not sure *I* want to talk to you. What were you thinking?"

He thought he heard someone else on the line. "Wait, is she right there? Belinda?"

His wife passed the phone to their daughter.

"Mom went to get some aspirin," Belinda said. "She has one of her headaches."

"You okay?"

"I'm fine, don't worry," she said. "I'm not really in shock. But seeing a woman get hit right in front of you isn't exactly routine. But she's making too much out of this. As usual."

They spoke for another thirty seconds or so and then she said she'd better go because "I'm being told I need to go lie down. Which is absurd."

Just before they hung up Belinda whispered, "Did you get it?"

MICHAEL ARRIVED HOME LATE. He slept in the den on the couch, the watch cupped in his hands.

He woke up several hours later in the dark.

He remembered a dream:

The woman of white, her face a bloody mess, rose from the depths of a swimming pool to strangle him.

He took Belinda to the city hospital the next afternoon.

"I STILL DON'T SEE why we're here," she said as they sat in the waiting area. "I mean, we don't actually know her."

"I want to make sure she's okay."

"I bet you stole it. And now you're giving it back, aren't you?" Belinda glared at him, then picked up a magazine and began flipping through pages, breathing heavily, making her disapproval known with little grunts and sighs.

CAROLYN LAY ASLEEP in her room in the midst of a labyrinth of tubes, hook-ups and machines.

Michael set the wristwatch on the dresser by the bed.

HE BROKE out in a cold sweat in the hallway, just beyond the double doors.

Belinda looked over at him from her seat at the end of the corridor.

WHEN HE REACHED HER, she stood up.

"I need to use the bathroom."

"Over there," he pointed.

Michael sat down and closed his eyes. A headache came on. He pressed his hands over his eyes, leaning forward. A throbbing pain, suddenly, a build up of tension; guilt; the poor woman of white; a memory in the past that meant so much to him; the moments of loss in his life; the damned vision of Belinda in her bathing suit rising from the waters of the YMCA pool with all those boys.

After a minute or two, Belinda returned and put her arm over his shoulder.

"Dad, it's okay. I'm not mad at you or anything," his daughter whispered. Her hands smelled of hospital soap and hand sanitizer, and she tweaked his ear slightly the way she often did when she'd been four years old.

A month later, closing in toward the holidays, Michael got a letter from a law firm claiming he'd stolen—from their client, Miss Carolyn Hoskins—an expensive wristwatch.

THE FIRM PRICED the watch at fifty thousand dollars.

"The value may be higher," the letter stated. "Our client believes the item is priceless."

He could only guess what had happened.

Carolyn Hoskins knew.

"Ha! That's *ridiculous*," Belinda said, after he showed her the letter. "They'd need to prove it. And she didn't even pay six hundred for it. They can check the receipt. What a scam. *Lawyers*."

They were both in the warm kitchen, a Saturday leaning toward noon. They shared a grilled cheese on rye and a bowl of tomato soup at the breakfast counter by the window overlooking the patio, which was covered with snow.

"Besides, you didn't take it," Belinda said, after she'd read the letter a second time.

"Someone else — a nurse, maybe a relative — must have stolen it. After I put it back," Michael said, pausing to take a sip of orange spice tea, one of Belinda's winter concoctions. "Of course, she thinks I did it. She saw me pick it up."

"Oh come on," Belinda said. "Nobody's going to remember that after they get hit by a truck while lying in a hospital bed all doped up. Her lawyer probably got your name and address from the cops. She just *thinks* you did it. What a greedy little piggy she turned out to be." Then she added, "And remember? She said she needed five thousand bucks."

"I don't remember that at all."

"I do. She said she wouldn't sell it to you for five grand. Well, now we know her price. What a con artist."

"Not sure what the next move'll be," he said, setting the letter down by his plate. "I guess I'll need to shoot a note back about that damn watch."

"Why'd you even take it back in the first place?" Belinda asked.

"I was wrong to steal it."

"If she died, she wouldn't have cared."

"But she didn't die."

"But she might've."

Michael cocked his head to the side, looking at his daughter's face.

"Is this the kind of stuff the debate team argues about?" He waved his spoon in the air as if making a point.

Belinda ignored the question. She picked up a paper napkin and leaned over, wiping up some of the soup spatter on the front of his shirt. She frowned slightly at the result.

"Well, it's a mute point now."

"You mean 'moot point'," he corrected.

"No, I mean mute. She can't say much about it. She doesn't have any evidence. You saved her life. You sat with her in the ambulance for god's sakes."

"That doesn't change the issue. Or this letter."

"Maybe not. But when I die I don't care if someone takes my red shoes," she said. "And I love these shoes. I'd fight for these shoes."

"But wouldn't you care who'd get them?"

"Not if I'm dead. They can have at them. They can set them on fire if they want."

Michael narrowed his eyelids. "This person is not dead."

"She's seriously injured, Dad. She may slip into a coma or something. Anything could happen. And you're out your watch."

He bit down on his lower lip. He should've told her by now why they'd hunted for that watch. It seemed too late. What was the point?

"It's not my watch," he said. "It never was."

"It is, *too*," his daughter insisted. "You want it. As long as I've known you, we've been looking for it. She doesn't need it. Not if she dies, anyway."

"Belinda, I don't like this kind of talk."

"It's not like you didn't think about it. If she died, what does she need a watch for? She wouldn't care."

There was more to his little girl than Michael had ever realized. He wondered if she'd misinterpreted all those little chats and negotiations while they sought their treasures — the coins on the beach, the sulfite marbles, the amethyst glass bottles, the onyx elephant, and *the watch, the watch, the watch.*

They're just things, he wanted to say but felt this wasn't the moment to get into it. *Things.* Nothing more.

"So, now it's okay to steal?" he said.

She shook her head. "No, that's wrong. If someone's alive. But I'm talking about if she died. A watch would be pointless to her. What's time mean to someone who's out of time?"

"But could you live with that?"

She shrugged. "Maybe. If I'd been hunting for that watch since the world began. Like you have."

"Stealing from the dead, Belinda?"

"Don't forget, *you* stole from her in the hospital. So don't get all judgy when it comes to this."

"I was stupid. It was disgusting what I did," Michael said. "I feel terrible about it. It was my reptilian brain that did it. Pure impulse."

"Don't knock the lizard brain," Belinda said. "You saved her life. And probably mine. You got the ambulance and went with her. She should be thanking you. You've got zero to feel guilty for."

"I don't agree."

"Listen," his daughter said leaning in to twirl her spoon in the soup bowl. "Remember that red granite lion? The one in the British Museum. And all the other stuff. Did Lord Carnarvon really care that he was raiding tombs?"

"Well," Michael said. "It was a long time after

King Tut died. Maybe if you give someone a few thousand years, a little thievery's forgivable."

"In fact, isn't it true that Lord Carnarvon and Carter and their team of thieves did the mummies good? They made King Tut famous all over again. We all love Egyptian history because of thieves. And don't even get me started on the Elgin Marbles."

"You might want to consider the legal profession," he told her.

They joked back and forth about the various museums built on theft from one group or another, the wonderful kingdoms built on extortion and skullduggery, the terrible De Medicis and the fantastic Renaissance (with Belinda reminding him yet again that he would never see the Uffizi), about auctions themselves being a kind of tomb plunder.

"I bet that watch shows up at auction again," Belinda said. "Maybe we can get it, after all. Maybe it'll go cheap this time."

"You miss the part where I'm being sued?"

His daughter shook her head slightly, as if he were being an absolute fool of a dad.

"It's not a lawsuit, dad," Belinda said. "It's a shakedown. She's lying there in the hospital. Her bill's astronomical. She needs money. She got some ambulance chaser to send it. Don't be afraid. What can she prove? Who'll believe her? Who's going to even back her story?"

A week or so later, days away from Christmas, Michael saw the obituary in the paper.

"CAROLYN HOSKINS," he said the name three times.

"Who?" His wife asked as she went to grab her purse from the coffee table.

He glanced up. "Oh, that woman. The one who got hit."

"The one who's suing you?" Belinda asked.

"She died," Michael said.

"You're being sued?" His wife stopped in the middle of the room.

"Not anymore," Belinda said.

His wife glanced at their daughter with a mysterious expression. "I'm always the last to know in this house."

"She was in her late thirties," Michael said. "Unmarried. New to the area. They'll do the funeral back in Chicago."

"I thought she was much older. And such a long way from home," Belinda said. "Does it say what she died of?"

His father looked over at her. "I'm sure it was the accident."

"Poor thing," Belinda said. "How awful. God. *God.* We should send flowers, Dad. We really should.

Something bright and hopeful. Not the usual funeral stuff. Or maybe there's a charity. We should do something. Really."

After her mother went upstairs, Belinda settled down beside Michael on the sofa.

She tugged the newspaper from his hands.

"SUCH A DINOSAUR, STILL READING PAPERS," she said.

"I like the feel of newsprint."

"Like I said, dinosaur." Belinda folded the paper over and read the obituary silently.

When she finished, she said, "That's so sad. Dying is just not something I ever want to do if I can help it. But, I suppose, we all end up there. Eventually. Such a terrible, terrible thing to happen. I take back all those horrible things I said about her. Poor lady."

She reached over and picked up Michael's cup of coffee. Lifting it to her lips, she checked to see if he disapproved. Took a sip, made a face, put the coffee back down on the coaster.

"You must feel a little better, Dad."

"Not really."

"I mean, because of the lawsuit."

He thought a moment. "Maybe. I guess that's all in the past."

Belinda leaned back, one leg over the other, head on the cushion as she flipped through the rest of the paper.

"Isn't it weird, Dad? We spend years looking for this particular watch, right?"

He nodded.

"It's something you really, really want. Ever since I can remember, you talked about the watch."

"It was a little crazy, I guess."

"So we find out about the auction for some old stuff, and — *voila* — here's the exact watch. Right nearby. And then this woman outbids you. Only she gets hit by a truck. And then you take the watch when she's in the hospital, but you feel bad about it. So you return it the next day. And sometime after that, someone else steals it."

Belinda took a deep breath. "It's almost like she wasn't meant to have it."

"I guess we weren't meant to have it, either."

Belinda laughed. "That's not what I'm getting at. What I mean is, maybe the watch didn't want her. *Fate*."

"Well, poor Carolyn. Not a great fate."

"Yeah, if only she'd sold you the watch in the first place. She'd probably still be walkin' around with her white coat on."

Michael thought no more about this until Christmas Day, when Belinda pulled him aside after all the presents were opened, after stuffing themselves on eggnog and pie, and after his wife took the dog out for a walk in the snow.

Belinda drew him into her bedroom.

SHE PATTED the edge of the bed. Michael sat down.

She wore her Christmas red sweater and gray sweatpants. Her feet were bare, toenails painted frosty pink.

He noticed — for the first time — that no pop star posters remained on the walls.

Belinda shook her hair out and then drew it behind her ears so it wouldn't flop in her face. She wore the small diamond earrings they'd given her that morning.

From behind a pillow, she brought out a wrapped box.

"More Christmas?" he asked.

"I didn't want Mom to see it."

"A secret?"

"Kind of." She shrugged.

Belinda passed him the box.

Michael looked down at it. He undid the knot of silver string, tearing the neatly folded paper with its red and green snowflakes.

"Dad, remember how you once said to me how fate doesn't just happen — you have to make it?"

Opening the slats of the cardboard box, he saw a gently curved glimmer of silver.

Oh, Belinda, he thought, looking at her intensely. Eyes like pond water, faint freckles, barely perceptible dimple in her chin. He felt as if someone kidnapped his child and put this girl — a replica, a changeling, almost Belinda but not quite — in her place.

"You stole it?" he whispered as he held the watch in his hands.

"No guessing," she said.

But several other guesses began streaming through his mind as he thought of the events — of *fate* — of the woman in white so hesitant to step out into busy traffic, Belinda with that rolling motion of her hands standing behind Carolyn Hoskins and mouthing a word — *Fate? Hate? Wait?* — reaching out to pull the poor woman back at the last second before she went into the path of the truck.

But had Belinda really tried to save her?

Michael imagined his daughter stepping forward and pushing the woman of white into traffic.

Impossible.

He looked at his daughter — really studied her face, as if he'd never taken the time to see her. Not as a little girl but as an adult slowly emerging from some outer sheath of innocence while boys in *Speedos* watched her and as a woman in a hospital bed looked up to see a teenage girl grab a watch from the dresser, a girl whose father sat in the waiting room thinking his daughter had gone to use the restroom.

Had she returned to the hospital later, after the letter arrived? Had she pushed a pillow on Carolyn's face, unplugged machines, or done any of the dozen things you could do to stop the life of someone who couldn't move much, who went in and out of consciousness, who lived on a morphine drip?

No, she wouldn't. Ridiculous. She's smart and stubborn and she can make your head spin with those moods of hers, but she'd never murder someone.

What kind of father are you to even think it?

But that memory of Belinda in the pool, the way she paused near the top of the ladder as she let her luxuriant hair fall from bathing cap to shoulders.

He'd seen her glance at the boys — for just a second.

As if she knew what she was doing to them.

Enjoying the power.

Unlike the girl he'd raised. Unlike the daughter he knew.

Who was she?

Who had she become?

What was she capable of?

"Belinda," he whispered, holding the watch in the palm of his hand. He could barely get the words out. "How'd you get it?"

"I'll tell you. After you tell me something."

"All right," he said, breathing slowly, trying not to imagine.

She slid back, up against the headboard, drawing her knees toward her chest.

"It's something I've never understood — all these years."

"And then you'll tell me how you got this," he reminded her, the sense of an undertow in the room.

"Sure. Right after."

Belinda rested her chin in her hands, her elbows atop her knees, looking up at him with that sense of wonder she'd never quite lost from childhood.

"So, Dad," Belinda said. "What's this watch really mean to you?"

ABOUT THE AUTHOR

Douglas Clegg is the *New York Times* bestselling and award-winning author of *Neverland*, *The Priest of Blood*, *Afterlife*, and *The Hour Before Dark*, among many other novels, novellas and stories. His first collection, *The Nightmare Chronicles*, won both the Bram Stoker Award and the International Horror Guild Award. His work has been published by Simon & Schuster, Penguin/Berkley, Signet, Dorchester, Bantam Dell Doubleday, Cemetery Dance Publications, Subterranean Press, Alkemara Press and others.

A pioneer in the ebook world, his novel *Naomi* made international news when it was launched as the world's first ebook serial in early 1999 and was called "the first major work of fiction to originate in cyberspace" by *Publisher's Weekly*, covered in *Time* magazine, *Business Week*, *Business 2.0*, *BBC Radio*, *NPR*, *USA Today* and more. His book *Purity* was the first to be published via mobile phone in the U.S. in early 2001.

He is married, and lives and writes along the coast of New England.

Find the Author Online:
www.DouglasClegg.com

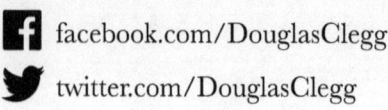

facebook.com/DouglasClegg

twitter.com/DouglasClegg